RUNAWAY PONY

Runaway Pony

Previously published as *Runaway Radish*

by JESSIE HAAS
pictures by MARGOT APPLE

SCHOLASTIC INC.

New York Toronto London Auckland Sydney
Mexico City New Delhi Hong Kong Buenos Aires

For Ann Tobias

ISBN 0-439-76155-7

Text copyright © 2001 by Jessie Haas. Illustrations copyright © 2001 by Margot Apple.
All rights reserved. Published by Scholastic Inc., 557 Broadway, New York, NY 10012,
by arrangement with Greenwillow Books, an imprint of HarperCollins Publishers.
SCHOLASTIC and associated logos are trademarks and/or registered trademarks of Scholastic Inc.

12 11 10 9 8 7 6 5 4 3 2   5 6 7 8 9 10/0

Printed in the U.S.A.   40

First Scholastic printing, April 2005

Originally published in hardcover as *Runaway Radish*, 2001

CONTENTS

CHAPTER 1

Judy

When Radish was a round, red, bouncy young pony, his little girl's name was Judy.

Before he got Judy, Radish lived on a big pony farm. He ran and played with the other ponies. He learned to go fast. He learned to think for himself.

A trainer taught Radish to let himself be ridden. She was a good rider. Radish had to do whatever she wanted.

Then Judy's parents came to the farm. "We want a pony for our little girl," Judy's father said.

"Radish is my best pony," said the trainer. "He's smart and he's brave. But he does have a mind of his own."

"So does Judy," said Judy's mother, and they brought Radish home to be Judy's pony.

Judy was small. She couldn't make Radish do anything. Most of the time she couldn't even catch him.

Radish liked that.

He liked the carrots Judy fed him.

He liked teaching her just where to scratch his neck.

And he liked scaring Judy, just a little.

Judy got bigger. Her mother taught her how to ride. Radish taught Judy other things.

He taught her the right way to fall.

He taught her to tie good knots.

He taught her to remember garbage-pickup day, and to keep her temper, and to hold on tight.

The more Judy learned, the bossier she got. She thought she could make Radish do anything. She thought she could ride just as well as the trainer.

Radish knew that wasn't true. He just waited, while Judy yelled, and kicked him in the sides, and smacked him with the riding whip, and bounced in the saddle.

When Judy stopped having a tantrum,
Radish taught her something else. He taught
her that if she asked nicely, he would almost
always do what she wanted.

Sometimes Judy forgot to plug in the electric fence. Radish reminded her. So did the neighbors.

Judy was sad sometimes, and Radish let her cry on his shoulder. Then he breathed in her ear. That tickled, and made Judy smile.

Sometimes Judy wanted to go fast and far and get away from everybody. Radish was the best pony in the world for that. Sometimes he went even faster and farther than Judy wanted.

"That pony thinks he can solve every problem by running away," Judy's mother said. "We should take him to a trainer."

Sometimes Judy agreed. Sometimes Radish made her so mad she cried.

But Radish was good sometimes too, and the more Judy learned, the more often he was good.

Every summer they went for rides in the woods and orchards, and every summer the rides got longer. They won ribbons in the horse show. They swam in the pond. Radish was the diving board.

Every winter, when the snow was deep,
Radish rested. Judy fed him and watered
him and took good care of him.

Winter lasted a long time. Judy read
horse books. Radish played with his ball.
They both watched the snow and waited
for spring.

But one spring when Judy got on Radish for the first time, she started to cry. She said, "Oh, Radish, you're too little!"

Radish was the same size he had always been. But now Judy's feet almost touched the ground.

"We look silly!" Judy said. She cried harder. She rode Radish in the woods, so no one would see.

For a whole month Judy didn't eat her vegetables. She fed them to the dog, one by one. Vegetables make you grow, and Judy didn't want to grow. She wanted to shrink.

But when Judy and Radish went to the horse show, the judge said, "You're much too tall for this pony. It's time you had a horse."

And Judy's parents bought Horton.

"I'll always love you best," Judy told Radish. She brushed him every day. She gave him even more apples than she gave Horton. And when Judy was sad, she still cried on Radish's shoulder.

But now it was *Horton* who took Judy into the woods. *Horton* won the blue ribbons. *Horton* went swimming, and Horton scared Judy, just a little.

Radish bit Horton, but Horton didn't care.

"Poor Radish!" Judy said. "I can't make you happy. You need a little girl, and I'm not a little girl anymore."

One day Judy put Radish in the horse trailer. She cried and kissed him. Then she took him to Nina's house.

CHAPTER 2

Nina

Nina was small. She couldn't make Radish do anything. Quite often she couldn't even catch him.

Radish liked that.

He missed Judy. He missed the apples and galloping through the orchards. He missed the way he could always tell what Judy would do next. He even missed Judy's bossy voice and her bossy ways.

But Radish wasn't sad. He liked the carrots Nina fed him. He liked teaching her
where to scratch his back. He liked hiding so
Nina couldn't find him, and he liked scaring
her, just a little.

Nina got bigger. She and Radish went to
riding school together.

The school taught Nina how to ride.
Radish taught Nina other things.

He taught her that puddles can be
dangerous.

He taught her how to jump.

He taught her to tighten the girth carefully, and to watch out for low branches, and to hold on tight.

Sometimes Nina didn't dare to go fast. She was afraid Radish might fall. She was afraid *she* might fall.

But going fast was what Radish loved best. He hardly ever slipped. He *never* fell. Nina never fell either, unless Radish wanted her to.

Radish showed Nina, and showed her, until Nina got braver. Finally she learned to relax no matter how fast Radish went.

Nina didn't like to clean stalls. She didn't like to soap saddles. She didn't like to get up early on weekend mornings, even to give Radish his breakfast.

But when Radish was hungry, he was cross. Nina learned to get up early every day. After a while she even learned to like it.

Nina was shy. She didn't like to do anything that would make other people notice her, not even win ribbons at the horse show.

But Radish liked people to notice him. He liked winning ribbons. He made Nina win whether she wanted to or not.

After a while Nina got used to winning. After a while she even learned to like it.

When Nina was lonely, she sat in
Radish's stall. She smelled his warm smell.
She listened to him eat. Sometimes she read
aloud to him. Radish loved books.

There were times when Nina *wanted* to
be lonely. Sometimes she hated everybody,
and they hated her too. Then she went
away on Radish.

They wandered along cool paths. They jumped over the brook. They listened to birds. They saw deer. Nina sat in a hay field and watched the clouds, while Radish ate grass.

Usually Nina felt better by the time they got back.

The more Nina learned, the more she dared to do with Radish. Every summer they went for longer rides, through the cornfields and down the dirt roads.

They climbed steep hills and slid down them.

They played gymnast. Radish was the balance beam.

They entered all the racing classes at the horse show, and they won too. One year they were champions of the whole show.

Every winter, when the air was cold,
Radish rested. Nina gave him water and hot
bran mash. She made him a thick bed of
shavings. She hung a Christmas stocking for
him. They watched the days grow longer,
and waited for spring.

But one spring when Nina got on Radish
for the first time, she said, "Oh, Radish!
You're too little!"

Radish was the same size he had always
been. But now Nina's knees were up by his
ears.

She felt heavy. Not *too* heavy. Radish was a strong pony. He could still carry Nina wherever she wanted to go.

But Nina was afraid she might hurt Radish, and so was Nina's mother. "Radish is too small for you," she said. "You need a big horse now."

And Count came to stay.

"I'll always love you best, Radish," Nina said. She gave him lots of carrots. She brushed Radish every day. She hugged him every time she saw him.

But now *Count* went on rides through the cornfields. *Count* went to the horse show. Nina didn't dare play gymnast on Count. Count scared her, just a little.

Radish tried to chase Count away. But Count was too big. He didn't even notice.

"Radish seems sad," Nina said. "And he's getting thinner."

"Radish is an old pony," said Nina's mother.

But ponies live a long time. Radish wasn't very old. He was just lonely.

CHAPTER 3

Lost

One sunny day Nina took Count for a ride. Radish wanted to go too. He was tired of staying home alone.

Radish whinnied after Nina and Count. He trotted up and down the fence. He leaned on the gate to watch them go.

The gate moved a little. Radish felt it. The gate wasn't latched.

Radish pushed harder.

The gate swung open.

No one was watching. Radish slipped through the gate.

He trotted down the driveway. At the bottom he stopped to sniff Count's tracks. They led downhill. Radish followed them, *clip-clop clip-clop* along the dirt road, all by himself.

The tracks went around the edge of a big cornfield. Far away, across the cornfield, Radish saw Count and Nina. Count was trotting fast. They were almost out of sight.

Radish had to catch up. He took a short-cut through the corn.

Crunch! went the stalks. Radish broke them and bent them.

It was dark and green in the middle of the corn. Over Radish's head the long leaves waved. Birds flew up out of the stalks. Mice jumped away down the rows.

The corn smelled good. But Radish was in a hurry. He bit off just one stalk and ate it as he trotted.

Radish went as fast as he could. He didn't stop once. But when he got to the big road on the other side of the cornfield, Count and Nina were gone.

There were no tracks on the hard, black road. Radish sniffed it. All he could smell was tar.

Radish had been on this road with Nina lots of times. Sometimes they went one way, and sometimes they went the other. Before, Nina always had chosen which way to go. But Nina wasn't here now. Radish could go whichever way he wanted.

Radish looked to the right. Then he looked to the left. He sniffed the air.

To the right, the air smelled like Count.

To the left, the air smelled like something Radish couldn't quite remember. It smelled good, though.

Radish turned left. He tossed his mane and swished his tail. He started to trot, and then he trotted faster. It was good to be out on the road again.

A car went past. *BEEeeep!* Radish just kept going. He wasn't afraid of cars.

Dogs came out of yards and barked at Radish.

People stared out their windows at the pony trotting along all alone.

They called each other on the telephone.

They called the state police.

One woman said, "That's Nina's pony, Radish!" She tried to catch Radish with her clothesline.

But the woman couldn't run as fast as Radish could.

Radish went a long way. All the houses were strange. He didn't know the dogs. He didn't know the horses in the fields. He didn't know the trees or the garbage cans.

Radish was lost, but he wasn't afraid. The good smell was getting stronger, and now he knew what it was. It was woods, and orchards full of ripe apples. The smell made him think of Judy.

"Hey!" a man said, as Radish cantered past. "Isn't that Judy's old pony?"

The man ran after Radish. He took off his belt to catch Radish with.

But with no belt to hold his pants up, the man could not run very fast.

The smell of apples got stronger. Radish passed a house he remembered. He saw a horse he knew. Radish whinnied hello, but he didn't stop.

Then Radish saw a trail through the woods. Judy used to ride him on that trail.

Radish turned onto it. He was hot and tired now, but the woods were cool. He was getting closer. He trotted fast along the trail.

The trail led through an orchard. On some of the trees, the apples were ripe. They smelled good, but Radish didn't stop to eat even one.

Past the pond he galloped, and around the corner, and there was Judy's driveway!

CHAPTER 4

Found

Radish whinnied. He had hardly any breath left, he'd come so far and so fast. His voice sounded thin and wavery. But he galloped up the driveway.

The car in the yard was strange. The flowers in tubs by the front door were different.

But the house looked just the same as it always had.

A man and woman came to the front door. They looked at Radish through the screen. Radish had never seen either of them before.

"Goodness!" the woman said. "A pony!"

"Where did it come from?" the man asked. "What is it doing here?"

They didn't come outside.

Radish wanted a drink of water. He pushed at the screen door with his nose.

The people jumped back and closed the inside door too. They acted as if they were scared of Radish, just a little.

Radish shook his mane. He tasted the flowers in the tubs. They weren't very good.

Radish trotted around the corner to find his old stall.

The door was crooked. Spiderwebs hung in the window. The water tub was gone. Where was Horton? Where was Judy?

Radish sniffed the ground. He didn't smell Horton or Judy. He didn't smell himself. No horse had lived here in a long, long time.

Now Radish didn't know what to do. He took a bite of grass, but he was too thirsty to eat much. He was hot, and he was worried. He didn't want to be all by himself. Maybe he should go back to the pond and get a drink.

At last Radish heard hoofbeats.

Nina and Count came around the corner. Count looked hot and sweaty. Nina looked worried.

The man and woman from the house followed. They looked worried too.

"*Radish!*" Nina said. "I'm so glad to see you!" She jumped off and hugged Radish. "Mrs. Miller told me you went by. She said she couldn't catch you."

Nina put a halter on Radish. "Radish used to live here," she told the people. "He ran away—miles and miles."

"Amazing!" said the man.

A car came into the driveway. A tall girl ran around the corner. It was Judy.

"Radish!" Judy said. "Mr. Tatro told me you went past! I could hardly believe it!"

Judy hugged Radish too. She scratched his neck, just the way Radish had taught her. "I used to live here, six years ago," Judy told the people. "Radish was my pony."

"Amazing!" said the woman.

"Do you have a bucket?" Nina asked the people. "This pony needs a drink of water."

"Make sure it's warm," Judy told them. "He shouldn't have ice-cold water when he's this hot."

39

The people went away. Judy and Nina patted Radish.

"Radish isn't happy," Nina said. "He's too little for me to ride anymore. He isn't having any fun."

"Poor Radish!" said Judy. "It happened again, didn't it?"

"I guess he needs another little girl," Nina said. "I should try to find him a new home."

"But in a few years the next little girl will be too big too," said Judy. "Little girls always grow up."

Judy looked at Nina. Nina looked at Judy.

After a minute Nina said, "I wish Radish could have a home where he'd never be too little."

"Me too," said Judy. "But where?"

The people came with the water. Radish drank it all.

Then Nina got on Count again, and led Radish home. Judy drove behind them, flashing her lights. Radish went slowly. He was very tired.

Judy and Nina washed Radish with warm water. They dried him with towels. Nina fed him bran mash. Judy gave him a carrot.

"Radish is such a good pony," said Nina. "He made me brave."

"He taught me to be patient," Judy said. "He's the best teacher I ever had."

"I wish he could always have a little girl," Nina said. "Maybe we could find a family with lots of kids—"

Judy jumped up. "Oh! No, I've got a better idea! I'm going to go find out, and then I'll call you."

Judy hugged Radish. Then she drove away.

CHAPTER 5

Camp

Late the next afternoon Judy came back.
She had a woman with her. The woman
drove a pickup truck. A horse trailer was
hitched to the truck.

"This is Tish," Judy said. "She owns a riding camp. I just got a job there, and we need another pony."

"A good pony is hard to find," Tish said.

Nina led Radish out of his field.

Tish looked at Radish's teeth. She felt each one of his legs. She asked Nina to ride him around. Then Judy rode him a little.

"He seems strong and healthy," Tish said. "If he's as good a pony as you say he is, I'd be happy to have him at my camp."

"Radish is a *very* good pony," Nina said.

"Well," said Judy, "sometimes he's a bad pony. At least, he used to be."

"A good bad pony is the best teacher of all," Tish said.

"This seems like a good plan," Nina's mother said. "Do you agree, Nina?"

"Yes," Nina said. She smiled sadly.

Tish backed the horse trailer up. Nina put Radish's saddle and bridle into the truck. She hugged Radish.

"I'll miss you," she said. "Have fun."

Then Tish led Radish into the horse trailer. She closed the door. A minute later the truck started, and the trailer began to move.

There was hay in the trailer. Radish ate it. He listened to the cars and trucks on the road. Radish wasn't scared. He liked to go places.

When the trailer stopped, Radish could smell horses. Tish opened the door. She backed Radish out.

It was nearly dark, but Radish could see a barn, a big riding ring, and a pasture. There were horses in the pasture.

Tish led Radish into the barn.

Horses looked over the stall doors. They whinnied at Radish, and he whinnied back.

But Tish didn't let Radish stop. She put him in a stall. She gave him hay and water, and she left him.

In the morning Tish came back. Judy
came too. Judy fed Radish. She brushed him.
She scratched his neck.

Radish listened to the other horses. He
listened to other people talking. People led
horses past his stall door.

When Radish was all brushed, Judy put
on his saddle and bridle. Then she led him
out to the riding ring.

The ring was full of horses and ponies.
All the horses were much bigger than
Radish. Some of the ponies were bigger too.

A row of girls and boys sat on the fence.
The girls and boys were all different sizes.
There were just as many of them as there
were horses and ponies.

"Welcome to riding camp," Tish said.
"This morning I will give each of you a
horse to take care of while you're here."

"I want that big one!"

"I want the black one!"

"I want a fast horse!"

One by one Tish called the children. She gave them each a horse. Only Radish was left, and one girl, the smallest girl of all.

"Meg, you may ride Radish," said Tish.

Meg got slowly off the fence. She came toward Radish.

Meg was very small. She wouldn't be able to make Radish do much of anything.

Radish liked that.

Meg looked just a little bit scared.
Radish liked that too.

He put his head down. Meg patted
him. Radish turned his head and
showed her where to scratch his ear.

"You're in good hands," Judy told Meg.
"Radish has a lot to teach you."

All summer Tish and Judy taught
Meg how to ride.

Radish taught Meg other things. He
taught her that fly spray is important. He
taught her always to wear strong shoes. He
taught her how to dismount quickly, and to
keep her knees in, and to hold on tight.

The next summer, and the next, Meg rode Radish. The more she learned, the more fun she and Radish had. They went out for trail rides. They jumped over fallen logs.

They won ribbons in the camp horse show. They played broom polo. Radish was the best pony of all at broom polo.

In the winter the girls and boys went
away. They had to go back to homework
and piano lessons and basketball.

But Tish didn't go anywhere. She fed the
horses and watered them. She put them in
their stalls at night. She let them out in the
morning. She played music on the radio for
them. On Thanksgiving she made them a
big dinner.

Radish ran races with the other horses.
He watched the manure pile grow higher,
and waited for spring and Meg.

But one spring Tish said, "Meg, you're getting too big for Radish. This year Kevin will ride him."

Meg cried, and Kevin cried too. He was small. He couldn't make Radish do anything. Half the time he couldn't catch Radish, even in the stall.

Radish liked that.

After Kevin, Radish taught Sophie. Then he taught Pat. Then he taught Carlotta, and Robin, and Ginger, and Michelle.

By the time Judy's daughter, Rachel, was ready to learn, the riding camp was full of big girls and boys who had been taught by Radish. They all were brave. They all were patient. They all could tie good knots, they

never left the electric fence unplugged, and
they all knew how to hold on tight.

"Radish is a great pony," they all told
Rachel. Then they began to tell stories
about Radish.

"Remember when he bucked you off over
the stone wall and you lost your glasses?"

"Remember the day he galloped around
the ring with you for ten minutes straight?"

"Remember how he used to squish you
against the wall?"

Rachel held tight to Judy's hand. All her life she'd heard stories about Radish. All her life she'd wanted to ride him.

Now she was scared, just a little. She knew she was too small to make Radish do anything.

Radish knew too. And Radish liked that.

JESSIE HAAS

is a gifted and versatile writer of novels, chapter books, and picture books. Her many titles include the popular Beware series about Lily and her mare, as well as FIRE!: *My Parent's Story*, UNBROKEN, and WILL YOU, WON'T YOU? She is a graduate of Wellesley College and lives in Putney, Vermont.